OLD MACDONALD HAD A GOLF COURSE

BY KEVIN COLLINS
ILLUSTRATED BY JIM HUNT

TEACHER APPROVED Books ™

KID TESTED. TEACHER APPROVED.
HENCE THE NAME.

To Richard M. Collins, Sr.
a good golfer and a great grandfather.

Requests for permission to make copies of any part of the work should be mailed to:
Teacher Approved Books, 2140 Runnymede Boulevard, Ann Arbor, Michigan 48103.

First Edition
Kevin Collins
Old MacDonald Had a Golf Course / Kevin Collins; illustrated by Jim Hunt
p. cm.
Summary: After going hog wild on a spending spree, Old MacDonald and his animal friends transform the farm into a golf course in order to save the farm from mounting debt.
[1. Farm—Fiction.   2. Golf—Fiction.   3. Children—Caricatures and Humor.]   I. Title.

ISBN: 0-61-538661-X
ISBN-13: 978-0-615-38661-4

The illustrations in this book were done in ink and watercolor.
The type was set in Times New Roman.
Book design by Stephanie Armstrong.

Printed in the U.S.A.

Foreword

When I first read "Old MacDonald Had a Golf Course", I immediately connected to the story. I grew up on a farm in Australia and can appreciate Mr. MacDonald's fight to keep his pride and joy alive and to keep all of the animals happy and together. Times turn tough for Old MacDonald, so he comes up with a great idea of transforming his farm into a golf course so he can afford to keep the farm in his hands.

It's a truly great story that kids will love. Good values of helping others and teamwork are all throughout the story. It has meaning to my youth growing up with farm animals as a boy and now my life as a professional golfer.

Enjoy,

Stuart Appleby

Old MacDonald had a farm, E-I-E-I-O
With a chick, chick here, and a pig, pig there,
Old MacDonald had animals
Here, there and everywhere.

They'd all been living
High on the hog till
The day Old MacDonald
Got his credit card bill.

"ME-OH-MY, UH-OH!
Looks like we're in trouble.
I'd better call the farm animals
Right on the double!"

Old Mac broke the bad news
To the animals that afternoon:
"We're going to lose the farm
Unless we make some money soon!"

All the animals were scared,
Especially the little chicks
When the horse came up
With a really good fix.

"I've got it! I've got it!"
Whinnied the horse.
"How about turning the farm
Into a big, fancy golf course?"

One by one, the other animals
Decided to speak up too:
With an OINK, OINK here,
and a QUACK, QUACK there,
Here a BAA, there a BAA,
everywhere a MOO, MOO.

Old Mac said, "OKEY-DOKEY!
Let's give the golf course a try.
But first, we need to clean the barn.
This place looks like a sty!"

The animals cleaned
and cleaned
So the barn looked
spick and span,
While Old Mac put
on his thinking cap
And came up with a plan.

"The barn looks great,
But that's just the start.
If we're going to
build a golf course,
We'll all need to
do our part!"

The animals shook their heads
Every one of them agreed.
With no time to waste,
They took off in a stampede.

The cows trimmed the front nine,
As the pigs dug the sand traps.
The ducks made a water fountain
And the sheep knit the caps.

They all chipped in,
Working day and night
To make the holes not too long,
Not too short, but just right.

When Old Mac's course opened,
Each golfer got a lamb
To be their very own caddy
And get them out of jams.

Next golfers hit the greens.
They tee'd off at nine-thirty
With a swing, swing here,
a putt, putt there,
Here a par, there a par,
even a birdie, birdie.

Say you hit a bad shot
And had to yell, "FORE!"
It was no problem at all,
Because no one kept score.

And in between holes,
Why, that was the best part!
They rode around in the tractor
Instead of an ordinary golf cart.

Golfers came in foursomes
Braving the flies and manure
To make Old MacDonald's farm
The most popular course on tour!

It was the only place in town
Where nobody gave a darn,
If you went around acting
Like you grew up in a barn.

Then one afternoon while
The golfers played and played,
Old Mac went to the piggy bank
To count all the money they made.

"GOLLY GEE! YEE-HAW!"
He let out a hoot and a holler.
With a coin, coin here, a bill, bill there,
They'd made a fistful of dollars!

Business had been good.
They made more than their fill.
Now they could finally pay off
That whopping credit card bill!

Old Mac drove the fairways
Spreading the good word.
The animals came a-runnin'
As soon as they heard.

"You'll be happy to know that
The golf course worked like a charm.
We're finally out of the woods.
Together, we saved the farm!"

They celebrated that night by
Having a big barnyard dance
With a stomp, stomp here, a clap, clap there,
Here a spin, there a spin, everywhere a prance, prance.

And at the end of the golf season,
After the last golfer played through,
They went back to farming—
Just seemed like the right thing to do.

But to the animals' delight,
Life on the farm wasn't the same.
Old MacDonald still kept the driving range.
That way, they could work on their golf game.

What people are saying about
Old MacDonald Had a Golf Course

"Pigs and putters? Chickens and chip shots? Ducks and drivers??
Pretty ingenious stuff, mixing funny farm animals with golf.
This book is for active boys and girls with big imaginations—
in other words, every kid on the planet."
— *Dave Coverly, nationally syndicated cartoonist*

"A delightful tale of how we accept responsibility,
solve real problems and then, most importantly,
enjoy our solutions. This is a marvelous, imaginative story
of ingenuity in tough times, and the fun of friends working
and playing together. Suitable for children and adults alike."
— *John Barell, author and educational expert*

"Kevin has an inner sense that brings the rhythm, rhyme
and joy of childhood to a story. Thanks for sharing your gift!"
— *Tresa Squires, reading recovery specialist and teacher*

"Jim Hunt's illustrations are priceless! He has
breathed a whole new life into Old MacDonald."
— *Stephanie Armstrong, art director and designer*

"It made me laugh. It brought tears to my eyes.
It helped me shave two strokes off my golf game!"
— *Todd Blanding, avid golfer and father of two*

www.ingramcontent.com/pod-product-compliance
Lightning Source LLC
Chambersburg PA
CBHW041008170626
46815CB00002B/209